First published by Parragon in 2007

Parragon
Queen Street House
4 Queen Street
Bath BA1 1HE, UK

ISBN 978-1-4054-9568-4
Printed in China

Seahorse
Makes Friends

Illustrated by Sophie Groves   Written by Kath Jewitt

Bath · New York · Singapore · Hong Kong · Cologne · Delhi · Melbourne

Sam the seahorse was playing hide-and-seek
with his friends on the coral reef.

"Three...two...one...

Ready or not, here I come!" he cried.

Suddenly, there was a whooshing noise.

"Uh oh," thought Sam. "A big wave is coming.

I'd better get out of the way!"

SPLASH!

Before Sam could hide, a big wave crashed over the reef.

"Ouch," cried Sam, as he bounced over the bumpy coral. "Help!" he shouted, as he tumbled over and over in a big bubbly swirl.

When Sam finally stopped tumbling,
he opened his eyes.
Everything looked strange.

"This isn't my coral reef," he decided. "This looks like a tide pool, but I'm not sure."

Sam swam around to see if he could find anyone to talk to. But the tide pool seemed empty, so he sat on a shiny shell, feeling lonely.

"Do you mind?" snapped a voice inside the shell. "You're sitting on my house." It was a little hermit crab called Katy. "Sorry," said Sam. "I didn't think anyone lived here." Then he explained all about the big wave.

"Why didn't you say so before?"
said Katy. She clicked her claws loudly,
one...two...three.
"It's safe to come out!" she cried.

click

click

All at once, a lot of tide pool animals
appeared from their hiding places.
"Let's have a welcome party for my new
friend, Sam the seahorse," suggested Katy.
Everyone thought that was a good idea.

What a colorful party! There were orange starfish, pink
shrimp, red crabs, yellow and green sea anemones, and
shimmering fish the color of a rainbow.

"Wow!" gasped Sam. "Your home is just as colorful as my
home on the coral reef." Then he sighed a little sigh.

"What's the matter?" asked Katy. "Don't you like your party?"
"It's wonderful," replied Sam. "But I was just thinking about my friends at home. Do you think I'll ever see them again?"

"Of course you will," smiled Katy. "You just need to catch a wave home again. The tide is going out, so if you hurry you can get a ride at once. The fish will come along to show you the way."

"Bye, bye, everyone," cried Sam, as a wave carried him once again out of the tide pool.

"Bye, Sam. Come back any time. And don't forget to invite us to a party at your home one day," shouted Katy.

And that's exactly what Sam did!